Giving up is no alternative

AF285568

A. David Brown

Giving up is no alternative

Bibliografische Information der Deutschen Nationalbibliothek
Die Deutsche Nationalbibliothek verzeichnet diese Publikation
in der Deutschen Nationalbibliografie; detaillierte bibliografische
Daten sind im Internet über http://dnb.d-nb.de abrufbar.

© 2012 A. David Brown
Cover design, layout, production and publication:
BoD™ - Books on Demand GmbH, Norderstedt, Germany
ISBN 978-3-8448-2145-1

Chapter I

DOMINATION

Beware the dawn, for then the creatures stir
who make the world the way it shouldn't be,
and they are in control, can never err,

For they have wealth and, therefore, easily
manipulate the weak, who gladly yield
to the temptation of supremacy,

And bravely serve upon the battlefield
of might, on which their good is sacrificed
to politics and enterprise, their fate then sealed.

Beware the creatures laws, so well-disguised;
in truth, facsimile democracy,
because the real, for them, is stigmatised.

Their rule is destined for eternity,
unless mankind can overcome its fear
and implement nocturnal unity,
but who, of all of us, would volunteer?

According to Online Encyclopedia WIKIPEDIA, "a stroke, also called Apoplex or Insult, is a suddenly occurring illness of the brain which leads to a continuous malfunction of the central nervous system and through critical interruptions of the blood supply to the brain."

There are two forms of strokes which can be differentiated roughly by a sudden occurrence of a lessening of the blood supply to the brain (infarct) and an acute cerebral haemorrhage (insult).

~

For eight years I worked as an English teacher for a private Language school in Friedrichshafen at Lake Constance in southern Germany. The weekly courses lasted five respectively seven days and took place, either in Friedrichshafen in our classrooms, in hotels, at the customer's facility, or at the hotel in the vicinity. On the average we held about two to three courses per month. In addition we had to drive two to four hours both ways.

In 1995 we had an inquiry from a new customer, to offer seven day courses lasting from eight a.m. until ten p.m. with two breaks for meals and recuperation. I held several courses of this type until the last one from December first to the eighth, 1995.

In addition to the daily work load I experienced health problems, for example, high blood pressure which I occasionally had measured. I was determined to consult a doctor after this last course in 1995, however, it never came to it.

This is the story of three strokes which occurred within ten years to one person – to me. In order not to make this story too serious, I will tell of these occurrences partly in anecdote form. The way was and is not easy, however, at no time did I think of giving up and I still do not.

I hope that my story may help other patients to master their own misfortune.

Chapter II

THE ATTACK

Cerebral pain crept up on him
and stayed with him throughout the night,
increasing in intensity
until he rose.

It kept its strength, despite the pills
he took before the meal he'd had,
tormenting him as work began,
not letting go.

Then came the spells of dizziness
that cancelled out efficiency,
causing him to sit down and rest,
although in vain.

A numbness hit his body's right,
disabled arm, and hand, and leg,
preventing that he grasp or hold,
or that he walk.

The speed with which the doctor came,
the ambulance transported him
to hospital for urgent care,
kept him alive.

The battlefield of the attack,
his body that was now debris,
could only be rebuilt in years,
with his resolve.

And so he asked what he could do
and did it without wavering,
thus helping those, who had the skills,
to heal and mend.

He never will forget that day,
aware it could have turned out worse,
and yet his greatest fear is that
it come again.

It was the last day of such a seven day intensive course for that year.
The day started with headaches that did not let go of me and followed
me into the classroom.

When we began our relaxation exercise, I noticed that I also had pain
in my right arm, which became worse. After this relaxation we had
physical exercise, playing ball. Directly after this, I allowed the participants to go for a coffee break, while I attempted to put my CDs in
their covers. Since the CDs fell out of my hand several times, I realized
that something was wrong with me. I, therefore, asked one of the class
members to inform the manager of the hotel and that she call the
emergency doctor. The participant then helped me to my room. Before
the doctor arrived, I phoned my wife and assured her that everything
was okay, which, of course, she did not believe.

When the doctor came he asked me, first of all, for my health insurance card. I searched for it in my pants pocket, however, I could not feel it. Only when they undressed me at the hospital did they find it. The doctor realized immediately what was wrong with me, he ordered an ambulance and, when it came, the driver asked me which hospital I wanted to be taken to. I said: "to the nearest".

The ambulance took me first to the hospital in Überlingen and then for a computer tomography to the hospital in Singen. The result was a burst aneurysm which had caused bleeding within the Thalamus region of the brain.

Back in the Überlingen hospital, I spent the weekend in intensive care. There was one situation which, when looking back, troubled me greatly. My wife told me that I had spoken a mixture of German and English to the doctors and nurses and had apologized to them for it.

Chapter III

HIS PART OF RECOVERY

The natural abilities,
the ones he took for granted,
were lost, no, taken from him,
he had to retrieve them.

His motivated attitude,
the will to do his utmost
had helped to start the healing,
the pain, though, was constant.

With energy and enterprise,
in contrast to his nature,
he soon was making progress,
small steps, taken slowly.

His tenacious perseverance,
and optimistic outlook,
helped overcome the setbacks,
and work to tomorrow.

With importance in relation,
and humour rediscovered,
and time deprived of meaning,
his part was accomplished.

On Monday December 11, 1995, I was transferred from intensive care to a normal station. I was then in a three-bed room. First of all, I received a call from my oldest sister, a nurse in Scotland. The first thing I asked her was, "What can I do?" Thereupon, we worked out a program for me which moved all of my muscles and joints. In total we worked out fifteen exercises which took about thirty minutes. In the beginning we worked out fifteen minutes and, in time, we increased the number from ten to fifteen and then to twenty. I carried out this program three times daily for about twelve years.

The program:

Lying down:

1. Feet – paddling
2. Feet – fanning
3. Feet – circling (clockwise)
4. Feet – circling (counter-clockwise)
5. Right leg – bend and stretch
6. Left leg – bend and stretch
7. Right leg – set up, bend over left leg and return
8. Left leg – set up, bend over right leg and return
9. Set up the right leg and let it fall to the side
10. Set up the left leg and let it fall to the side
11. Set up both legs and let them fall separately to the side
12. Set up both legs an let them fall together to the side (left and right)
13. Build a bridge and hold for ten seconds
14. Build a bridge, lift and stretch left leg, and hold it for ten seconds.
15. Build a bridge, lift and stretch right leg and hold it for ten seconds

~

December 24, 1995

It wasn't our usual Christmas Eve. We should have spent it in the mountains, as we did every year, watching the winter sunrise in the morning, walking through knee-deep snow in the afternoon and listening to Christmas Carols by candle light in the evening. We should have, but we didn't, except for the latter.

My wife didn't come until after five p.m. that evening. She was carrying a large basket, which contained our dinner, bread, smoked salmon, cold cuts, etc. and a bottle of wine, also, two sets of our best china and crystal wine glasses. In addition she brought candles and a portable radio (see above).

We were given a small wreath with a candle in the middle, to decorate the only table in the room, a table just big enough for two. I had been in the hospital since December 8th. Diagnosis: stroke, bleeding in the Thalamus region (left side), resulting in paralysis, ataxia, and a sensitivity (touch) disorder on the right side of the body. Oh yes, and diabetes, which had just popped up with the stroke, but required insulin injections just the same.

As in most hospitals and clinics here, all patients that could be discharged for Christmas were, but I was not among them. Fortunately my roommate was, which left me with a single room for the entire holiday season. That is why my wife was allowed to have dinner with me that Christmas Eve. We cancelled my hospital meal days before, and she had a long talk with the Senior Consultant, to find out just what I was allowed to eat and drink.

When she had finished getting everything ready, the scene could not have been more beautiful, neither at home nor in the mountains. When we folded our four hands together to say Grace, it was more than just asking for our food to be blessed, or giving thanks for a meal. We knew all the things we had to be thankful for, beginning with the fact that I was still alive. It was a long silent prayer that ended with an audible "Amen", and tears in both our eyes. We lit the candle and turned on the radio. Within seconds, we were listening to Christmas music, hymns and carols. The meal was delicious. After all, what we were eating and drinking was not normally served in a hospital, at least not when the cafeteria was closed. After we had finished, I rolled my wheel-chair around to her side of the table. We held hands and listened to the music, both more relaxed than we had been since the stroke. A nurse came in and, in going out, she switched off the light. The view outside was marvelous – a winter landscape, a full moon, innumerable stars, and a few brightly decorated houses. We told the nurse to leave the lights off. The evening ended, as it had to, much too soon. But we were both certain that we had never spent a more beautiful Christmas Eve together, and perhaps we had come just a little bit closer to knowing exactly what the spirit of Christmas is, and what it means.

~

On Boxing Day, December 26, a new patient was brought to my room. He had had a stroke, however, he could not cope with it. On the first Saturday, on which he was with me, he asked me what day of the week it was. I answered "Saturday". He said: "Too bad, if today were a work day, the physical therapist would come". I replied: "What would you need him for? You could do what I do, do it yourself."

His reply was not surprising. He said: „No. The therapist is paid to do it."

On the day I was scheduled to go to Rehab, we said our good-byes to my neighbor, each in his own way. My wife preferred to give him a piece of her mind, concerning his behavior to others. He was very surprised and we left the room before he could react.

~

One very important part of my recuperation was my coping with the Diabetes which, as I mentioned, came with my stroke. For this purpose, we had one week training in coping with this illness. Although my blood sugar values were not so high, I still received insulin injections three times per day. For me this training was very educational, since we learned quite a bit from the other patients, for example, one of the patients did not take her situation quite seriously and, suffered an attack of hypoglycemia which she almost did not survive. She told me later that this was a very tough, yet educational experience for her. With such an experience, even if it were only hearsay, it makes one glad that it did not happen to oneself.

~

One of the most fascinating facilities in the hospital in Überlingen was an exercise pool in the basement. I went for a swim twice a week. The physiotherapist went with me to help me from my wheelchair to the lift. It was a wonderful experience to walk a few steps in the water with a little help. It was also nice that some student nurses were given permission to observe the exercises. They were very interested and asked very good and helpful questions.

~

Although, as a rule, a place for a stroke patient in a rehab center is applied for at the beginning of their stay in the hospital, this was, in my case, neglected. The intern who was responsible for this, was asked many times if he had heard anything about the application from the rehab center. This he had always denied. After six weeks the senior consultant proposed that they allow me to go home until a positive reply from the rehab center was received. After intensive discussions with my wife, we turned this proposal down. We were of the opinion that a stay at home could be too dangerous in my present health condition. After we had told the senior consultant of our decision, I accompanied my wife to the exit. Before we got there, a young intern came to inform us that the information from the rehab center had just arrived. The next day I left the hospital in Überlingen and drove with my wife to the Schmieder Clinic in Gailingen.

Chapter IV

INSIGHT

You look into an empty me
and wonder why there's naught to see.
Perhaps because the really wise
use more than just a pair of eyes
when searching for the gist of things
outside established reasonings.

The nothingness that you perceive
arises from what you believe,
and not from what is really there,
beyond your aptitude to dare
a comprehension of the whole
that constitutes a human soul.

The why of any being's state
is interwoven with its fate,
and must be fully analyzed
before it can be recognized.
That must be somewhat strange to you,
with your dogmatic point of view.

Gailingen is near the Swiss border, about fifteen kilometers from Singen west of Lake Constance. The Schmieder clinic is situated on a plateau, the main buildings are on various levels. House "Tirol" where I lived, is situated on a hill way above the other buildings. The inhabitants of House Tirol were not permitted to leave the house without accompaniment. This meant that we had no possibility to go to the café or any other building.

On my first day in Gailingen a young physiotherapist came to examine me to see what I could do and what I needed. The next day, we started the therapy but this time the therapist was not alone. For the next eight weeks I had two therapists at the same time. The problem was, however, that neither one explained to me, why we did certain exercises and what the exercises were for. In spite of this, the therapy was very successful. After eight weeks I was able to walk from House Tirol to the next building with accompaniment, of course.

∼

My favorite application in Gailingen, was actually ergo therapy, which took place on the top floor of the neighboring building. The therapy consisted mainly of the testing of the depth of sensitivity, the hypersensitivity of my right side by stimulation (brushing, ice treatment, etc.). Significant improvement in rump stability as well as selective movements of the rump were achieved.

∼

Because wheelchair patients were not permitted to leave House Tirol alone, we met each evening in the lobby in order to discuss problems, politics or simply difficulties we had, i.e. with doctors, nurses, therapists, etc. One problem that came up rather frequently, was our diet. Some of us received only ten to twelve bread units per meal. One evening my room mate was so hungry that he asked one of the 'mobile' patients to bring him a piece of cake from the café. Four additional patients joined him. When he had finished eating his cake, he complained that he was still hungry. Then a suggestion came from a further patient, to call a pizzeria in Gailingen and order pizza for all. The suggestion was unanimously accepted. This means that we had ordered sixteen pizzas. For understandable reasons, I did not order a pizza, although the temptation was there. We never ordered pizza again because a nurse told on us. Women!!!

~

At the beginning of the entrance to House Tirol was a door leading to the indoor swimming pool. Then came the doors to the dressing rooms and, subsequently to the pool itself. Although I had permission to use the pool unaccompanied, undressing and dressing before and after bathing was very strenuous. Nevertheless, it was at no time dangerous for me because there was always someone present, who could help me if necessary. I went for a swim practically every day and I enjoyed it very much.

~

Towards the end of my stay in Gailingen, I had the opportunity to take part in a seminar on the topic, "The Bobath Concept". The Bobath concept is a nursing and therapy concept for patients with paralyses (Parese, Plegien) and spasticity due to cerebral malfunctions: Stroke (apoplex), cerebral bleeding, SHT, hypoxic brain damage, brain tumor and other afflictions of the central nervous system."

Two therapists were assigned to me as well as to the other patients, or Guinea Pigs, as we called ourselves. After reviewing our medical histories, and interviews with us, the therapists formulated their goal for the week.

In the morning the physical therapists had therapists had lessons in Therapy and in the afternoon we were taught practical application.

The atmosphere was very pleasant and fun. I was very glad to be able to contribute to this atmosphere. The leader of this seminar came from England, which gave me a slight advantage. There was only one draw-back: my two therapists did not reach their formulated goal, which, however, had no influence on the total result.

For us patients the week was very interesting. We had gained a lot of experience and were able to compare and evaluate our experiences with our daily therapy.

By the way, when I arrived at Allensbach eight months later, one of the first persons who greeted me was one of my two therapists in Gailingen. It was a hearty greeting.

~

One part of the clinic staff had rehearsed a play which they wanted to perform. Unfortunately the performance was scheduled for the day of my departure. However, I was granted the opportunity to watch the dress rehearsal which I enjoyed very much because it left a lasting impression on me. My interest in the theater was later to play an important role in my recuperation.

~

Once per week, on Tuesdays, we sang folk songs in the top floor of House "Tirol". Everyone was in a good mood, and cheerfully joined in. It was a surprise to most of the patients that I, as an American, knew so many German folksongs. This made me actually very proud.

~

In the same room in which we sang folksongs, a protestant Church service as held on Sundays. My wife and I loved to take part because we had so many reasons to be thankful, especially for being able to be together.

Chapter V

FORTUNATE ME

Since my stroke, which I bear in civility,
people ask me, with some credibility,
how I am, how I feel,
does it not seem unreal?
I just answer in plain sensibility.

Oh, except for some slight disabilities,
which impair almost all my facilities,
I am feeling just swell,
working harder than ... , well,
to the limits of my capabilities.

I'm surprised at my new versatility,
which, when coupled with old durability,
helps me cope with it all,
often having a ball,
though I could use a lot more mobility.

Still, I'm grateful for tolerability,
motivation, strong will and humility,
and for humour, of course,
which is often a source
of relief and of mental stability.

On March 19, 1996, I could finally, after fourteen weeks, go home. The first few days were quite hectic. Since we had moved into our new apartment in Bermatingen only on the first of September, we had neither a new doctor nor the names of therapists nor other specialists I needed. However, my wife was able to find the names of doctors and therapists and had already made the necessary appointments for me.

First we had an appointment with Dr. Scheller in Bermatingen. She examined me with the emphasis on diabetes and, especially, on physical disabilities and disorders. Since we did not know each other, she had many questions concerning the history of my health. Among other things I mentioned that I have a twin brother. She became very excited and told me to inform him immediately that he might be in danger of having a stroke.

I explained to her that my brother was a professor for music at a small town university in the United States of America, where he led a very calm and pleasant life. Often, at the beginning of a semester, he complained that his teaching schedule would interfere with his golf and tennis games. Whereupon, Dr. Scheller was convinced that I wanted to say that there was no danger for my brother at that time, if at any time at all. Since then, Dr. Scheller has regularly visited and examined me and has become a reliable support for me and my wife.

~

Next, we found the physical therapist who would visit me at home, since my disability did not permit me to go to their office. Again, we were very lucky to find the office of a physical therapist here in Bermatingen. The first exercises were to maintain my mobility as well as stability. We used a Pezzi ball, sitting down and standing up, to increase the stability of my rump. Furthermore, we carried out exercises to maintain security in my daily life.

One day we exercised in the living room and I was very ambitious, so Petra, my therapist reminded me not to overdo it. I answered with the question: "Do you believe that I am ambitious?" Her reply consisted of only two words "And how!"

In addition we started to go for walks outside the house once a week. First we walked down two flights of stairs from our apartment holding on to the rail on the left side. When we got outside, I walked with the cane in my left hand while Petra stabilized my pelvis. My total walking time, including going down and up the stairs, was 60 minutes.

In June 2003 Petra discontinued working as a therapist, however, I will never forget and always be grateful for all she did for me. While I was writing this chapter she promised to help me. For this, too, I will always be very grateful.

$\sim$

Finally, I found an ergo-therapist in Friedrichshafen who turned out to be anything but satisfactory. One day, she tried to treat me and another patient at the same time in two different rooms, although we had two completely different medical histories. She kept hopping from one room to the other could not justify neither my nor the other patients needs. I was with her from April to November but I was actually glad that I had to go for my second rehabilitation to Allensbach and, therefore, could stop going to see this particular therapist.

$\sim$

During the early time at home, I tried to occupy myself meaningfully. This took the form of "killing time". My first efforts were PC games, such as Hearts, Solitair and Tetris. I tried to learn how to use the internet which was not successful at all because I was no fan of "surfing". I was much more successful with the production of greeting cards for special occasions, such as, birthdays, Christmas and weddings and simply amusing cards as reminders.

~

When I was in the hospital in December 1995, my twin brother and my older sister promised to visit me the following year 1996. The first one who came was my brother, who was very taken with the landscape and the people. Although he could stay only one week, his visit was obviously quite good for me. A few months later, my sister from Scotland came for a visit. She stayed a little longer and enjoyed driving to Friedrichshafen with me. And while I was in therapy, she went shopping. We also made some day trips to Austria, Bavaria, Switzerland and the Black Forest. Her visit did me well and I was very grateful that she was able to come.

Chapter VI

NIGHT THINKING

At times, I lie awake in bed, can't sleep,
and simply let my mind begin to roam
into the darkness of the night, go deep,

since only there, in meditation's home,
can answers to the whys of life be found,
and not within the pages of a tome,

regardless of its size or how it's bound:
the superficialities of sense,
by which the foolish value the renowned.

The silence of the dark becomes intense
and opens up my mind to cogent thought
prohibiting all tries at self-pretence,

and yet, the answers that I find are not
compatible with my expressed ideals
and can't disperse the grievous doubts I've got

that everything the human mind reveals
substantiates the way he truly feels.

In summer of 1996 I received permission to go for my second rehabilitation to the Schmieder clinic, this time in Allensbach. About one month prior to the scheduled date, I received a phone call from the clinic. The administration asked me whether I would be able to get along by myself in a single room. I said, of course I could well knowing, that I eventually might need help in certain things, such as while taking showers, or climbing stairs. However, I was very surprised when I realized how independent I actually was. I got along with a minimum of help during eight weeks of rehabilitation. My little white lie was necessary to give me the freedom I wished for.

$\sim$

On my first day I was treated by a physical therapist. Although he must have known that I had a severe ataxia in my right arm, he knelt down to examine my right leg. All of a sudden my right arm cut loose and hit him on his head and he fell down. Of course, I immediately apologized to him, nevertheless, we both had a good laugh and I am sure that we will not forget this episode so soon.

My first goal was to walk the few hundred meters from my room to the dining room by myself. First we selected a cane which I then used for seven years. We practiced short distances until I was able to walk the full distance by myself. It was very strenuous and I had to rest for two hours without lunch. The therapist was rather impressed and I was very proud because it gave me confidence for other goals I had set myself.

$\sim$

One supposedly important part of my treatment was speech therapy. In discussing this with a specialist we came to different opinions as what was the best for me. I was for individual therapy while the doctor preferred group therapy. The result was that I was together with a group of patients who had real speech problems, such as stammering, omitting or forgetting words. For this reason the therapist and I did not have enough time to concentrate on my problems. Too much time was wasted. However, this was the fault of the therapist who found it impossible to justly divide her attention, which lay more on the make-up of the group than on herself personally.

~

Since my rehabilitation in Allensbach was paid for by the BfA (a Federal Insurance institution for employees) they needed to determine when I would be able to return to work. For this purpose, I had to undergo a series of tests. To my great surprise, I was not able to successfully finish these tests, which made me very depressed.

Luckily these tests were supervised psychologically. The psychologist had a great understanding for my situation and helped me to see the positive side of things, i.e., that I should see the possibilities of the future instead of complaining about the unjustness of the present.

~

With me was also a thirteen year old patient from Muenster. Since his mother did not want him to be alone so far from home, she took a vacation for the length of her son's stay in Allensbach, so she took a room near the clinic. Because she could not afford to go to restaurant twice a day, she only went for lunch occasionally but never had an evening meal. When I found this out I offered to give her two slices of bread with butter and cold cuts, since I had four, although I could only eat two. The rest would have gone into the garbage anyway. She was very grateful and I believe that everyone would have done the same thing. Besides, it was a very good feeling to be able to help others.

~

As the 6th of December was approaching, I began contemplating whether I should distribute some chocolate Santas for "Nikolaus" day (December 6). I decided to do this, however, only for the nurses in our station and, also, for some of my co-patients. I asked one of the nurses to buy some chocolate Santas in one of the super markets near the clinic. On the eve of Santa's day I distributed the sweets in front of the nurse's office. Neither the nurses nor the patients ever found out who their "Santa" was. This was not important to me, I just had a lot of fun doing it.

Chapter VII

AGE

A person's age is just a number,
the sum of the years that he or she
has been on earth.

How old or young a person appears
depends upon how easy or hard
life was to them.

For shoulders and hands tell just as much
as face and skin, though never the same
to everyone.

What's known as beauty and viewed as youth
is nothing more than contentment seen
and acknowledged.

In the Spring of 1997, we started to take part in an English language
"Stammtisch" (a table for regulars) in a restaurant in Immenstaad. The
discussions were very informative and my wife and I enjoyed taking
part. In May, a few new members joined us. I noticed that they were

talking about a play they wanted to put on shortly. I joined them and showed my interest in taking part if they had something for me. The leader of the group was very interested and suggested that I could put together the music for the production. He invited me to take part in the next rehearsal on the following Sunday. I gladly agreed.

The rehearsal took place in the beautiful garden of a private home near Heiligenberg, where the later performance was planned. During the rehearsal, I leafed through the book and read a role where it was not clear, whether this person was standing, sitting or walking. I told the director that I was ready to play this part if it were free. The director was happy to give me this role for which nobody had applied yet.

After a few weeks we were ready. Much to our regret it rained very hard on the day of the performance, so the production was not possible in the garden and we had to move to the town hall of Wintersulgen. The performances were very successful anyway, this gave our group the confidence to officially register it for theatrical productions.

First we had to find a name for our theater group and we decided on the name "The Bodensee Players". The next step was to elect a board of directors. As I did not want to become chairman, I let myself be talked into becoming vice chairman.

The decision as to which production we were to put on next, was very difficult but we finally decided on the comedy "The Bride And The Bachelor". The next decision was a little more difficult. I was asked if I would be willing to take over as director of the play. After a brief deliberation, I agreed to do this, which I never regretted.

The rehearsals took place in the theater "Kaserne" in Fallenbrunnen, a suburb of Friedrichshafen.

During a rehearsal, when I was in the back of the theater, one of the actors on stage said something I did not agree with, I ran with my cane without thinking to the actor on stage to give him my opinion. Every one was surprised that I had done this, since I usually stayed in my seat and rarely came to the stage.

The closer the time for the performance came, the more nervous some of the participants became. Up to the dress rehearsal, nobody knew how the sale of tickets was going. However, on that day we found out that the greater part of the tickets had been reserved. With great joy we were looking forward to our first performance. On the day of the opening performance we experience a great surprise. The performance was not only completely sold out, we even had to provide additional seats. The performance was a very great success. In addition to the scheduled performance for the next day, the owners of the theater offered us an engagement for three additional performances.

Our next production were two one-act plays on one evening: "Womberang" and "Last Tango in Little Grimley". I directed the "Last Tango". The big difference to the former production was that the large theater was not available. Instead we had to use the so-called "Atrium", which had a maximum capacity of only one hundred seats and a much smaller stage. Despite that, both plays were very successful. It was decided that for the next production to put on two more one-act plays, among which was the sequel to "Last Tango". With my understanding, another member of the group was chosen to direct.

In spite of everything I had the feeling that I no longer belonged to the group. It was, as I said, only a feeling but it disturbed me. For this reason I rarely went to rehearsals and, in the end, never. In discussions with committee members, I got the impression that most of them would be content to see me leave the group, since in their opinion I was, with my fifty-eight years, too old for this group.

Chapter VIII

THAT OTHER GUY

Because that other guy was born
just seven minutes after me,
I had to fight, in many ways,
for what I wished to have or be.

My life, to me, was nothing less
than competition with a ghost
who always won, or so it seemed,
and that was that which hurt the most.

And so, I left to find my world,
to be myself, to start anew.
I wound up with a lasting love
and many dreams we made come true.

Our worlds were rather far apart,
perhaps is that one reason why
my feelings are much stronger now
for him, my twin, that other guy.

In August 1997, one of my cousins arranged a family reunion of the Brown family, i.e. those of the generation of my father still living and their descendants. We flew from Friedrichshafen to Frankfurt and then to Boston. The first few days we stayed with my younger sister before we moved to my twin brother's house in Amherst. But first my brother had arranged for a great surprise for me: he had two tickets for a baseball game of the Boston Red Sox, my favorite team in my childhood. We had seats, i.e. my brother had a seat and I my wheel-chair.

For the first time since 1957, I was back in Fenway Park, the home of the Red Sox. The game was so good and so exciting that I really enjoyed the whole afternoon. By the way, the Red Sox won 5:2.

The following Monday we drove to Amherst, about 2 ½ hours. My brother's house was on corner property with quite a few coniferous and deciduous trees. It had a double garage through which we entered the house directly into the kitchen. Then followed the dining room and next the living room. The bedrooms were off the hallway left and right. At the end of the hallway was my brother's office. We loved this house, it was so cozy and very convenient to move around with my wheel-chair.

The time in Amherst flew by so fast and most of the time was spent shopping and browsing through the large shopping centers and the marvelous book stores near Amherst. One of our favorite stores was the Yankee Candle Company, founded by a young man who made his first candles in his mother's kitchen. Business was booming and still is.

~

On Saturday August 23, 1997, we met the Brown clan, i.e. the descendants of my grandparents, at the house of one of my cousins in Ware, MA. There were about 80 relatives, including 5 brothers and sisters of my father. Of course we did not know most of the younger members, however, it was great to see the brothers and sisters of my father. Some of them I had not seen for over 60 years. It was only due to my resemblance with my father, that some even recognized me at all.

The day went by, as such days do, much too quickly, but it was very nice, although I knew that we would never see the majority again. That is why I am very grateful that we had the opportunity, despite my handicap, to meet so many relatives, known and unknown.

~

On the last day of our vacation we had quite a lot to do, mainly packing. We found out that we had bought too many things and did not have enough luggage space. Although it was Sunday, the shopping center in the neighboring town. We drove over, bought a suitcase and had a typical American meal for lunch.

Chapter IX

THE VISION

I'm sitting at my study's desk,
a pad of paper lies prepared
to take down all the notes I'll write
when simple thoughts become ideas.

I feel them stir and make their way,
then reach out with my strong right hand,
to grasp upon the writing tool
with which I start to tell my tale.

And when I need a reference book,
I lay it near me, on my left,
the fingers of that less-used hand
will turn the pages while I write.

I see it all, as it should be,
the way it was, but is no more,
and realise it cannot change
no matter how I wish it to.

Ataxia will never leave
and give me back the usage of
my hands to write with pad and pen,
or any other finer task.

And so the vision takes the place
of ever being able to,
and though there's pain in memory,
forgetting is more painful yet.

As I realized that my time with the "Bodensee Players" was slowly coming to an end, I tried to find a new occupation for my free time. At this time I remembered that my mother always wanted me to become a writer. Although I had occasionally written poems for company day trips, Christmas parties and such, these were only for entertainment and not really meant to be serious.

Only after serious deliberation over eventually trying to become a writer or poet, I started to write short poems. I asked some of my English and American friends what they thought of them. Their reaction was definitely positive and that is why I decided to continue writing seriously.

Because I was not sure whether I wanted to write poetry or short stories, I decided to take a correspondence course with the London School of Journalism in short story writing, at the same time continuing my poetry writing. I was surprised how easy it was for me to write short stories, especially, when my tutor claimed that the openings were very good and very interesting. The course was very rewarding and I noticed how I was able to write better and better. I was really able to put myself in the shoes of my characters. The course lasted one year, however, I extended it for an additional six months in order to get more experience.

A very important decision before publishing was the question as to "where?" For this purpose I purchased two books from Amazon, "The

Poet's Market" and "Novel & Short Story Writer's Market". I really studied these books seriously and found publishers in the USA and England. I submitted several poems and short stories and waited. In the meantime, one of my poems, "Delusion", was published in December 1999 in "The Poet's Voice", a publication of the University of Salzburg (Austria). The first of my short stories, "The Night Clerk" was published in the winter of 2000 in "The Storyteller", a writer's magazine in Maynard, Arkansas, USA.

During the first six years I wrote more than 400 poems, of which 70 were published in the USA and Britain, and of the 63 short stories, seven were published. In addition, two of my poems and two short stories were short listed in competitions. In another competition, my poem won and in another it became second. In the year 2004 I wrote 101 poems. In the years 2005 to 2009 I wrote a total of 31 poems. Because of the increasing ataxia during the past years, I was no longer able to feed myself, let stand doing any writing. Although I could not write any longer, I still entered various competitions, mainly for poetry.

In the summer of the year 2008 my brother wrote to me that there is a park, the Armstrong-Kelley Park, near his summer house on Cape Cod, MA, with an exhibition of flowers and plants, sponsored by the Cape Cod Horticultural Society. In this exhibition a circular path has been laid on which tablets on wooden posts display poems by famous poets. My brother had inquired whether they would also accept poetry from lesser known poets. After several months of consideration, the society said yes. My brother then submitted one of the poems I had sent him and after several months I received a positive reply. A few months later my brother sent me photos of this section of the park and I was very proud to see that one of my poems was displayed.

$\sim$

Chapter X

LONGING

High on a ridge on the Cornish coast,
above its rocks and waves and beaches,
a winding path, a cliff-side walk,
commands my view.

More than a mile of descending slope,
that levels out, then climbs a little,
reminds my heart of other trails
from other years.

Hikers appear and arouse in me
an urge to join them in their pleasure,
relive a time of can and will
that used to be.

As they approach, the longing deepens,
a sadness comes, begins to torment,
I turn and look to where they'll be,
try not to weep.

After they're gone, I wait for a while,
then roll to the car, my wife assists me,
I get inside, she stows the chair,
we drive away.

In 2002 my wife would celebrate her 75th birthday and we our 40th wedding anniversary. For this occasion I wanted to do something special for my wife. Since my wife was an avid fan of Daphne du Maurier, Victoria Holt and Rosamunde Pilcher and therefore, fascinated by the county of Cornwall, I decided to book a fourteen-day vacation in Cornwall. My wife was ecstatic and we found a travel agent in Hamburg, who specialized in trips to Southwest-England i.e. Cornwall. We decided on a small cottage in Carbis Bay, a suburb of St. Ives.

Saturday, April 27th:
Herr Sterk, with his wife, drove us to the airport in Zurich. Then we flew to London, to Heathrow airport, where we had a delay waiting for a hydraulic lift truck to get me off the plane, but we had a very pleasant conversation with the captain (Texas tie pin) and the crew. When we finally reached the terminal to get our luggage, Marianne, who had flown from Cologne to Heathrow, was waiting for us there. Together, we then took a bus from Heathrow to Gatwick (£ 35 – 39 miles), where we had to wait about three hours for our flight to Newquay. We flew with a very small plane (Dash - 800), which was quite loud, but not uncomfortable.

In Newquay, we picked up our rental car, a Rover 45, which they told us was larger than what we had requested, but it wasn't large enough for us to get all our luggage and the wheel-chair into it without problems. While we were struggling, the rain got heavier. By the time we finished, it was pouring. Then we started our drive south. After a few involuntary detours, we finally got onto the A30, and headed for St. Ives. It rained the whole way, and Inge's having to adjust to driving on the left-hand side of the road didn't make it any easier.

In St. Ives, Inge hit the curbing with the front, left tire, which produced a flat. We finally found a garage that was open, the attendant called his boss, who called a mechanic, who came and replaced the flat with the 'space saver'. Then he told us to come back on Monday, when he would have a new tire for us.

We then drove around, trying to find the house we were to stay in for the next two weeks. Luckily, we met a man out walking his dog (in that weather?), and he directed us to the home of Clatworthys ('Oh, you mean the plumber'). As Inge started to help me get out of the car and into the house, I slipped and fell, and pulled her down with me. I merely bruised my right elbow, but she fell full force with her right shoulder and the right side of her head against the stone wall of the house. Besides bruises and abrasions on her back and shoulder, she also split her right ear-lobe, which Marianne, luckily, pressed together, to keep it from separating, then cleaned it up and bandaged it.

We found a surprise waiting for us in the kitchen. There was a packet of three sorts of Cornish clotted-cream short-bread (plain, chocolate chip, and raisin) and a greeting card for our fortieth wedding anniversary. It was signed, 'Margaret and Malcolm', and although our anniversary wouldn't be until mid-July, we felt it was a wonderful gesture from the owners of the cottage. Inge had told Mrs Clatworthy the reason for the holiday – the anniversary – and she must have assumed it was at that time.

After we had brought the luggage into the house, Inge and Marianne drove back to town to do some shopping, so we could have something to eat. The only store that was open was the Spar market in St. Ives, but that was sufficient. When they returned, we had a late, light snack in the kitchen and then went to bed.

Sunday, April 28:

We slept late – 9:30 – and then had a good breakfast. After we got cleaned up, dressed, and organized, which was about noon, we went over to the main house to meet our landlords, Margaret and Malcolm Clatworthy, who unfortunately were having brunch. We also met their dog, Oliver, a mixture of Collie and Spaniel.

After a light lunch, we took a long nap, as we were still quite tired from the day before. Later that afternoon, we drove over to St. Ives. The Spar market was opened, which Inge and Marianne knew, so they did some more shopping for food for the next week or so.

When they were finished, we drove down to the shore, where we found a parking space, amazingly, and then took a short walk. The rain shortened it for us. Since it was dinner-time anyway, we went into a pub, The Sloop Inn. It was a typical English pub, which meant we had to order at the bar and bring our drinks to the table ourselves. The bartender brought us the food when it was ready. Inge and I had roast duck – more like a vegetable platter with a side order of duck. It was excellent. Marianne had fish.

After dinner, we drove around St. Ives, looking at the buildings, the homes, the beaches, and the shore. Around nine, we drove home. At ten we watched the news, world and local (Devon and Cornwall), then went to bed. This was to be our routine almost every night of our holiday.

Monday, April 29th:

In the morning, we slept late, had brunch, and took our time getting ready and dressed. Then we drove over to the garage, which was on the main road, just a few yards from where Laity Lane (where we were staying) begins, to get the new tire. It took about an hour before they got it and put it on.

Afterwards, we went down to Carbis Bay beach and enjoyed just sitting on the wall, looking at the waves. Then we drove over to St. Ives, to Tregenna Castle, to find out if Marianne could play golf on their course. The people at the castle sent us over to the course, where we were told it was for members only, but there might be a possibility of playing at The West Cornwall Golf Club in Carbis Bay. We drove over there, but found no one to ask, so we began looking for a place to have dinner. We ended up at the 'Cornish Arms' on the main road between St. Ives and Carbis Bay. It was also a typical English pub, like the 'Sloop Inn'. Inge and Marianne had Chili, and I had liver (?). We all enjoyed our meals. When we were finished, we went back to the cottage and relaxed until news-time.

Tuesday, April 30th:

After breakfast, we drove up to the Cornish Goldsmiths near Portreath. First, we went into the 'Gold Centre', saw the workshop, where a goldsmith was working on a piece of jewelry and then spent quite a while looking at the gold jewelry in the showroom. There was almost too much to see. We had coffee and cake in the cafeteria and looked at the James Bond exhibit – film posters, an Aston-Martin sports car, and a 'Beatles' VW-Beetle, covered with pennies.

Then we went through the Tolgus Tin Stamping Mill and Steam Works, which has been restored, so that many parts are operating again. Before we did, we saw a video of the history of tin mining in Cornwall and of the Tolgus Mill itself. It was fascinating. After the tour, we had a long talk with the attendant and learned a lot more.

Finally, we visited 'Cornish Silver', a combination exhibition and retail shop, similar to the 'Gold Centre', but without the workshop. Inge bought two silver ball-point pens with Celtic signs on them, one for herself and one for Frau Sterk, and a silver book-mark, also Celtic, for me.

Instead of going directly back to the A30, we drove in the opposite direction, to Potreath, where we spent some time at the beach, before heading for home. On our way back, we missed the exit to Carbis Bay and wound up at the round-about just before Penzance. Because of this, we got our first view of St. Michael's Mount. It was magnificent, so we made a mental note to return there soon to take a closer look.

We found the right way back to the cottage and had chicken pies for supper, after which, we took it easy, read and relaxed, until it was time for the news.

Wednesday, May 1ˢᵗ:
We woke up to sunshine, the first really sunny day since our arrival. We, therefore, got up early, had breakfast, got ready, and drove off. First, we drove through St. Ives, onto the coastal road, which took us to Zennor, Morvah, and Pendeen. The road was narrow and winding; we never knew what to expect behind each bend: cliffs, the sea, the shore, or more of the rugged landscape. It was fascinating and reminded us of pictures we'd seen of the Irish and Scottish coasts, rocky and bare.

Shortly before St. Just, we turned right and drove to Cape Cornwall, a peninsular of steep grassy slopes, ending in cliffs above the ocean. The car park there is administered by The National Trust. When the attendant asked if we'd like to become members, we said we were from Germany. "That's all right," she replied, "We'll take anyone."

Off to the right, the path led down to the base of a hill and then up the hill to a monument. Marianne walked over to the base of the hill, but not up to the monument, while Inge walked around the edge of the cliff. I sat in my wheel-chair on the grass next to the car, watching the waves, the seagulls, and the lighthouse not far away.

To the left of the car park, across a wide gorge, was the steepest, hilliest, and most rugged golf course I had ever seen. Nonetheless, there were several players there, trying their luck. Marianne commented that a lot of golf balls must land in the ocean.

When we left Cape Cornwall, we drove back to the coastal road, then through St. Just and Sennen, heading towards 'Land's End'. Between St. Just and Sennen is a small airport where trips to the Isles of Scilly can be booked and taken.

Next, we drove from Sennen to Land's End. The closer we got to Land's End, the more signs we saw announcing, "The Last *Something* In England": "The Last Petrol Station In England"; "The Last Bed & Breakfast In England"; "The Last Pub In England", etc.

Land's End is, on the one hand, a sort of theme and amusement park, where they have multimedia shows, computer- and other games, a souvenir and gift shop, a post office, and, of course, a huge self-service restaurant, with picnic benches set up in the square in front of it, which is surrounded by the other buildings. We parked the car at the disabled car park and had lunch at one of the picnic benches. Then we went around to the back and discovered that, on the other hand, Land's End is a breath-taking view of the landscape, especially the cliffs with the cliff walks, the shore, with the waves rolling in over myriad rocks, and the ocean stretching all the way out to the horizon.

At the Land's End signpost, the three of us had our picture taken together by a professional photographer, who promised we'd get them within a week.

We then walked down to the 'First and Last House'. There are three paths, parallel to each other, that can be used to get to it: the highest path slopes steadily and gradually all the way down to the house; the second path is steep going down at the beginning, levels off in the middle, and is steep going back up at the end; the third path is even steeper at both ends and has a suspension bridge over a gorge in the middle. Needless to say, we took the first path. But no matter which path one takes, the view is worth it. In the end, we had to pull ourselves away, when it was time to go, and just barely managed to.

At the gift shop, we bought some souvenirs, as well as some post cards, which we had stamped at the post office. When we were finished, we drove home to Carbis Bay on the A30, by way of Penzance, and spent a pleasant evening at home, having sandwiches for dinner, reading and relaxing, before watching the news and going to bed.

Thursday, May 2ⁿᵈ:

After breakfast, we went over to Hayle, where they have a golf driving range and a short course (12 holes), as well as an eighteen-hole course. Marianne was interested in taking lessons, but was told that there was no possibility of doing that in the area. When we got back home, Malcolm just happened to come by, so we asked him if what Marianne had been told was true. He said no, and that she should try at The West Cornwall Golf Club, where he is a member, which she did.

Later, we decided to go to the Trevarno Estate Gardens and the National Museum of Gardening in Crowntown, near Helston, about 25 miles due east of Penzance.

The first thing we did, after we got there, was to visit the gardening museum, which was very interesting, with an amazing number of exhibits showing the development of gardening tools and equipment – e.g. lawn mowers – over the ages.

When we were finished, we went over to the Fountain Garden Conservatory, a huge sort of winter garden with a restaurant and a gift shop in it. In the middle of the room is a very large fountain, surrounded by potted plants and trees. At the back, there were glass doors opening onto a typical English lawn, rather large, upon which were two female peacocks. We had lunch while enjoying the atmosphere and observing the peacocks.

When we left the conservatory, we saw two workshops in the building opposite: a soap workshop and a herbal workshop. Only the soap workshop was open. We went in and observed a young man cutting, weighing, and packing soap.

Afterwards we started walking around the estate, following the 'Map For The Disabled', which we had been given at the gate. Opposite the Conservatory lawn was another large lawn also with a peacock on it, male, extremely beautiful, and painfully loud. The way around the estate was very beautiful; the trees, plants, and flowers were just fascinating. But, although the map said the path was suitable for wheelchairs, it was so steep in places, that either I had to get out and walk, or Marianne pulled the chair and Inge pushed it, while I remained seated. It was frustrating for me.

We did get to feel the contentment of sitting on a park bench above the pond, watching the 'Glistening Cascades' of the stream fall into it and just enjoying the surroundings. But I could not go any further down to the pond, because there were only steps there. In fact, we had gone as far as we could go, and had seen everything we were able to see, anyway, since, as we discovered in the end, only about one-third of the paths are accessible by wheel chair. So, despite the natural beauty of the gardens, and our satisfaction with what we did see, the Trevarno Estate Gardens were a big disappointment for me.

Finally, we drove home, rested a bit, and around 6 p.m. drove to the Badger Inn in Leland, the town next to Carbis Bay going East, for dinner. The setting was perfect, the food was excellent (I had roast pork, served from a carving table), and the waitress was quite good, although I got the impression she was rather new to the place. We had a very pleasant evening, before we drove home, watched the news, and went to bed.

Friday, May 3ʳᵈ:
We took a day off. In the morning, Inge and Marianne did some housecleaning and some laundry, while I read my book (Ken Follett's, "Code to Zero"). In the afternoon, they went shopping – big shopping – and went over to The West Cornwall Golf Club and booked a lesson for Marianne the following Wednesday, while I continued to read.

In the evening, we drove to St. Ives, looking for a place to have dinner. We parked the car at Porthgwidden Beach car park, and, while Inge was helping me out of the car, Marianne found a very nice restaurant, The Porthgwidden Café, right at the end of the car park, above the beach. It was cute, and the food was great. We had a magnificent view of Porthgwidden Cove, and I watched a sea gull, sitting on one of the rocks, silhouetted by the setting sun. It sat there for a long time, and I thought of writing a poem entitled, "The Lonely Sea Gull".

Saturday, May 4ᵗʰ:
Shortly after breakfast, Adrian Martiensen, who had helped found The Bodensee Players in Friedrichshafen, and whom we had notified immediately after we decided to make the trip, called to make arrangements for us to meet that afternoon in Marazion. He and his wife, Alice, had booked a flat there so they could see us again, and spend some time with us.

Then we got ready, drove down to Carbis Bay Beach and just enjoyed sitting there, watching the waves come in. It was peaceful and quiet, although there were a few people – young and old – playing games, building sand castles, etc. Marianne took a long walk, down to the water and along the shore.

Shortly after we arrived, the car's alarm went off, and then, after a while turned itself off. When we decided to go home, we discovered we couldn't start the car. While Inge and Marianne went to the hotel, to inform Europcar, I read the manual and learned how to correct the malfunction. When they returned, I told them, but the AA had already been called, so we decided to wait. It was just as well we did. The AA man gave us a number of tips and told us a few things about 'our' Rover that made us certain we would never rent one again and would never again rent any car from Europcar. Because of the extra time lost due to the incident, we had no time to take a nap, but plenty of time to get ready and drive to Marazion.

Adrian and Alice met us at the car park in Marazion, and we first took a walk along the beach – it was low tide – before they led us to the flat they were staying in, which was only a short walk away, where Alice's mother, Joan, was waiting. The flat was on the first floor of the house and had a magnificent, unobstructed view of St. Michael's Mount from the lounge.

We had a drink (Gin-tonic, among others), coffee, tea, and an amazing amount of conversation – reminiscences, etc. – before we went out to dinner at 'The Godolphin Arms' hotel, which was just down the street. Unfortunately, Alice's mother was not feeling well and decided not to join us. We understood: after all, she was ninety-two.

The meal and the evening were excellent. Before we parted, we arranged to meet again and take a tour of St. Michaels Mount. Adrian said he would try to get permission to drive over, taking me and Alice's mother, since the way is too difficult to walk, and too rough for wheelchairs.

Sunday, May 5th:

The day was beautiful; we had sunshine from the beginning to the end. After breakfast, we drove down to Penzance and parked the car at the huge car park at the harbor. First we walked down, past the harbor, to the War Memorial. I had wanted to go into town to see the Egyptian House, but the road seemed too steep for me to walk, or for Inge to push the wheelchair. So Marianne left us at the War Memorial and went up to see if the strain would be worth it. While she roamed around town for the next half-hour, we looked at the War Memorial and the huge swimming pool complex – the Jubilee Pool – next to it, which however, was empty of both water and people, since it was closed. When Marianne returned – the strain would not be worth it – we started back, had a Cappucino at a street-side café, went window shopping through a closed shopping center, and after picking up the car, went on our way.

We then drove over to Mousehole, where the streets were so narrow, that Marianne, who had insisted on doing the driving that day, was completely unnerved by the time we found a car park. So, instead of parking the car and taking a walk, her only thought was getting out of Mousehole as quickly as possible, which, of course, was no more quickly than getting into Mousehole had been. However, we managed to find the way out and onto the road to Land's End.

On the way, we stopped near a field, in the middle of which stood a circle of huge stones known as the Merry Maidens. The car park was too small – five cars at the most – the gate was closed, so you had to climb over the embankment next to it in order to get to the field, and there were neither signs nor any other sources of information to explain just what the site was: a rather disappointing tourist attraction. However, we were compensated for it by what we saw at our next stop.

The Minack Theatre is a wonderful, huge, old amphitheatre built into the face of a cliff, near Porthcurno. Because of the buildings – administration, coffee shop, gift shop, and museum – and the steepness of the cliff, neither the theatre nor the stage can be seen from outside. Besides, there is a fence built around the accessible parts of the complex.

First we visited the museum, which told the story of Rowena Cade, the founder and original builder of the Minack, and, with photographs, scale models, and audio-visual displays, showed how the Minack came into being and had developed through the decades of the twentieth century.

Afterward, we went out into the theatre. It was breathtaking. I couldn't go down any paths or steps, of course, they were much too steep. So I stayed in my wheelchair, with Inge, of course, in the disabled seating area at the top of the theatre, while Marianne went all the way down to the stage to look around.

While we were there we saw actors rehearsing for the opening production of the season, "Orpheus In The Underworld", to be presented in two weeks time, starting May 20.

We did not visit the coffee shop, but we did get some souvenirs – and a battery for Inge's camera – at the gift shops before leaving and driving down to Land's End, where we missed the exit at first, but finally got on the A30 to go home, where we had quiche for dinner and a very pleasant evening

Monday, May 6th:

The weather was not quite as good as on Sunday, rather overcast, but we decided to take a trip over to Falmouth (approx. 30 miles) to visit Pendennis Castle. We didn't leave until two o'clock in the afternoon, but we had plenty of time, or so we thought. But we missed the exit in

Redruth, which would have been the direct way, and wound up having to drive all the way to Truro, before turning down to Falmouth.

Unfortunately, when we arrived, we didn't realize there was a car park on the castle grounds, so we had a long and strenuous walk from where we did park – and back. Fortunately, there were many friendly people (that is an understatement) along the way, who helped us with me and the wheelchair.

On the castle grounds was a huge tent, inside of which was a fair, showing goods and services, arts and crafts, from all over Cornwall. We decided, however, to walk around the grounds first, before going into the tent to see the fair.

At the far end, there was a tower, which Marianne went up to see, while Inge and I stayed down and roamed around. There was a large display of armaments on most parts of the grounds. We could see, when we were at the tower, that the tent detracted terribly from the picture of the castle grounds. Although, as we soon discovered, the fair was very interesting, we felt it was a good thing that it was only a one-day event.

When Marianne rejoined us, we walked over to the coffee shop, where we sat outside, although it was quite windy, but the hot coffee did us good. After that, we browsed around the gift shop, took it easy going back to the car park, and drove home by way of Redruth, thereby avoiding a repeat of the early afternoon's detour.

As we drove through Carbis Bay, Inge noticed that what we thought was just a Fish and Chips take-out was also a restaurant. Since we had not yet had Fish and Chips, we decided to go in. The entrance opened onto a bar-lounge, where you could order, then have a drink, and be shown to your table, when your order was ready. There were three dining areas, decorated with paintings by local artists. The food was delicious, the service was excellent, and the prices were quite reasonable. We knew we'd be returning there before flying back home.

Tuesday, May 7th:

We woke up to beautiful blue skies and sunshine. It was to be the last sunshine we would see on that day; the clouds covered the skies before we could sit down to breakfast. After breakfast, Adrian called to give us instructions as to what to do when we arrived at the Eden Project. We left the cottage around ten minutes to ten, since I had told Adrian we would meet them at the project between eleven and eleven-thirty. As soon as we got on the road, it started raining and continued to do so all the way. The closer we got to the Eden Project, the heavier the traffic became. Shortly before we got there, Adrian called – on Marianne's cell phone – to tell us they were on their way and that they would meet us at the entrance. By the time we got onto the grounds, we were going at a snail's pace. We asked the attendant the way to the disabled car parks, of which there were three (!). One can imagine then, how many there were for the non-disabled.

When we had parked the car, we got the wheel chair down to the entrance with the help of a friendly visitor. Unfortunately, the admission area was over-crowded. An employee of the project explained that, because of the rain, the 'bios' were practically full to capacity, so they were slowing down the admission of visitors. She suggested we sit down in one of the cafeterias and have a cup of coffee, which we did. While we were waiting, Adrian called again and told us they were waiting in the queue to buy tickets and that they would be over in a while. When they came, we had a warm greeting, they got coffee, and while they drank it, Inge and Marianne went to buy our tickets. When the coffee was finished, the tickets bought, and everybody ready, we went outside and began our tour of the project.

In the 'biops', it was extremely interesting, but also rather hot and humid. The trees and plants grew so high and thick in places, that we sometimes had the feeling we were on safari somewhere in the jungle. Although there was a waterfall and flowing water, there was also an air conditioned cabin at one point along the way, so that those who needed it, or thought they did, could cool down for a moment. Since the 'biops' had been built against the far wall of the clay pit, the paths climbed steadily higher, in a zigzag pattern, leveled off for a short distance, and then began to climb again. Wheelchairs were not allowed to go up the final ascent, to the very top, so we did not get to see the magnificent view from there.

Where the path was too steep, upwards, I had to get out and walk, arm in arm with Marianne, or she pulled the wheelchair, while Inge pushed; where the path was too steep, downwards, as it was in the beginning, on the way down to the 'biops', I had to get out and walk, arm in arm with Marianne, while Inge pushed the wheelchair. Either way, I wasn't able to concentrate as much, or as well, as I'd like to have. Be that as it may, we had a very good time the others were fascinated by everything they saw, especially Alice's mother.

When we had seen the first part of the 'biops', we went over to the next part on a walkway, that looked down on the restaurant, which was very full. So we decided to continue our tour. All plants at the Eden Project are beneficial to mankind, as food (e.g. bananas), raw materials (e.g. hemp for rope), building materials (e.g. bamboo or wood), etc. There were many practical examples throughout the project.

When we did go to lunch, we had various little things, such as a bowl of soup or a baguette. We decided to take the small train back up to the entrance. Since the train also has to drive zigzag and takes about fifteen minutes, we had a magnificent view of the entire project. Large sections of the outside area had yet to be planted, but that would take time, we were told.

Finally, when we reached the top, we left the train and walked back to the car park, said our good-byes – knowing we'd see each other on Friday, in Marazion – and then drove home, where we had sandwiches for supper and spent a pleasant evening.

Wednesday, May 8th:

This was our second day of relaxation, but first, after breakfast, we drove to St. Ives to do some shopping and mail some post cards. We parked across the street from the Spar Market, and while Marianne did the shopping, Inge went to the Post Office, a few yards down the street, and I waited in 'The Harbour Bookshop & Gallery', directly in front of which we were parked. It was a small shop, but it had a very large selection of books. There was even one section of paperbacks devoted entirely to fiction that takes place in Cornwall. When Inge came to pick me up, we gave in to temptation and bought much too many books, but then again, when would we ever get a chance like that back home?

In the meantime, Marianne had finished shopping and returned to the car, so we put everything we had bought into it and drove around to the car park above and between Porthgwidden and Porthmeor beaches. We parked and then walked down the road until we found a way onto Porthmeor Beach. We walked through the sand, which wasn't easy for me, until we came to a group of rocks that was the boundary of the beach on its right side. There were a few bathers lying on towels or blankets, or sitting on them, with their backs against a rock. We did the latter, with rocks of our own choosing. We watched the tide coming in, swimmers trying to surf, children playing ball, and fishing boats passing slowly by. We saw and heard seagulls scolding us because we were obviously too close to their rocks. We also read the newspaper, watched the clouds floating overhead, or just relaxed. When the time was up, we walked back to the car. The way was steep and strenuous for me, but the memories of that morning were worth it.

When we got home, we had lunch, after which, for only the second time in ten days, Inge and I lay down and took a nap. Marianne wasn't able to because she had a golf lesson over at The West Cornwall Golf Club, but when she got back, she joined us, so to speak. We must have still been tired from the day before at the Eden Project, since we didn't get up until somewhere between five and five-thirty that afternoon. Then we had coffee and apple pie, after which, we sat outside the kitchen talking. At one point, Margaret came around, and we chatted with her for awhile.

Later, around seven-thirty, we decided to go to the fish-and-chips restaurant again. This time it wasn't as crowded as it had been on Monday. Inge had a bowl of soup, Marianne had prawns, and I had fish cakes – delicious, but much too much. Although, there must have been some room left over somewhere, since we all had banana cream pie for dessert.

Thursday, May 9th:

After breakfast, around noon, we drove back up to 'Cornish Silver' to buy a decorative wine-bottle cork for Herr Sterk, and a miniature silver tin smelt as a souvenir for our glass case in the living room. Interesting was that the shop assistant recognized us from our visit there ten days before and even remembered what we had bought. It must have been my wheel chair.

After we left 'Cornish Silver', we drove through Redruth and took a country road – the B3297, which was very narrow in places, but the countryside was lovely – down to Helston. From there, we took a broader road – the A3083 – down the Lizard to Lizard Point. At Lizard Point, we parked the car and walked down the somewhat steep slope to a small restaurant, which was more like a snack-bar. We all had turkey sandwiches and sat outside, although it was very windy. After I'd finished my Sprite, I had to stick my knife handle in the opening of the tin, to keep it from being blown off the table.

When we were finished, Inge and Marianne went further down the slope – which was much too steep for me in that part – to where there was a gift shop and a stonecutter's shop. The stonecutter made ashtrays, candle holders, lighthouses, etc. out of serpentine stone, which he cut and polished himself. Inge bought an ashtray for Marianne and two candle holders: one for Christoph and one for Thomas. Marianne bought a candle holder for us.

While I was waiting at the restaurant, I savored the view of the ocean, the countryside, and the cliffs. I watched people coming down the cliff walk from a distance, and I thought back to the times I liked to hike. I longed to be able to go on such cliff walks.

When Inge and Marianne came to pick me up, we climbed back up to get the car, and then drove around to the Lizard Point lighthouse. We didn't go up the stairs inside, of course, but we did sit on a wall outside for quite a while, just admiring the scenery.

As soon as we were able to pull ourselves away, we drove back home, stopping first at the supermarket in St. Ives, where we bought some ready-to-serve meals for supper – macaroni and cheese for me, green noodles and sauce for Marianne, and a chicken and bacon flan for Inge – as well as several other items to eat and drink (e.g. Baileys, to last until we had to leave). After supper, we had a pleasant evening, just talking and reading.

Friday, May 10th:

We got up a bit earlier, because we had arranged to meet Adrian, Alice, and Joan in Marazion at ten o'clock. We got there at a quarter to ten, but that was no problem, as the others arrived shortly thereafter. I got into Adrian's car, where Joan was already sitting, and Adrian drove us over the causeway to St. Michael's Mount, while Alice, Inge, and Marianne walked.

After we had parked the car, and the others had arrived, we walked around to the entrance to the castle. The way was quite rugged and Inge had to push the wheelchair onto the grass, where she could, and I got out and walked, when she was no longer able to. We decided that it would be too strenuous for Joan and me to go up inside the castle, and Inge said it wouldn't be best for her, either. So we went into the castle courtyard, where there were tables and chairs belonging to the cafeteria. After Adrian, Alice, and Marianne went back to take the tour of the castle, Joan and I took our seats at a table in the courtyard, and Inge went into the cafeteria and got scones and clotted cream for each of us, plus creamed tea for herself and for Joan, and apple juice for me. We had a wonderful conversation, chatting about this and that until the others came back from their tour of the castle, which they all said was very, very interesting.

The three of them went into the cafeteria and got creamed tea and scones, the same as we'd had, then joined us outside at the table, and told us about the tour. Then we all went into the castle's gift shop, where Inge, Alice, and Marianne took the chance to see a video show, there, about the castle, while Adrian and I browsed around the shop, before going back to the courtyard and Joan. When the others returned, they told us how impressive the video show had been. Inge had bought some souvenirs: painted post cards, not only of St. Michael's Mount, but also of Cape Cornwall, and a postcard-sized picture book entitled, "Cornwall's Coasts".

Looking at the time, we realized we had to leave St. Michael's Mount quickly, because the tide was beginning to come in. So Adrian drove us – Joan and me and Inge – back to Marazion. When we got there, we parked the car and went over to the quay wall to watch Alice and Marianne walking back, but when we reached it we saw them directly below us, at the base of the wall.

Alice and Marianne then bought some cakes, before we all drove over to Carbis Bay, where we had coffee/tea. We also showed Adrian, Alice, and Joan the cottage where we were staying. Then, around three, it was time for us to say good-bye, since they had to go back to Marazion and pack for the long journey home the next day. Besides, it had been a very long day for Joan.

After they had left, Inge and Marianne began packing for our long journey home the next day. Since I could have been of no help anyway, I finished my book. When everything was packed, they wanted to drive over to St. Ives to get some money and look for a restaurant where we could have dinner. But I was not feeling like going into St. Ives, so they went alone. When they got back, we decided to go to the fish and chips restaurant one last time, although we all said we were not hungry. We had a delicious meal: Inge and I shared a steak that was served with chips, fried onion rings, and green peas, and Marianne had fish and chips, but no dessert.

After we got home, we watched the ten o'clock news and, afterwards, went straight to bed since we had to get up so early the next morning.

Saturday, May 11th:
Time to go. We got up very early, at half-past six, and had breakfast, cleaned up the cottage (Inge and Marianne), got ready, finished the

packing, and loaded the car. Then we had the difficult task of saying good-bye to Margaret, Malcolm, and Oliver. Inge and Marianne took pictures of the three of them. At the end, Malcolm said, "Good-bye, my friend," to me, which made me feel very good.

We then left and drove to Newquay airport. Surprisingly, we had no problems, whatsoever, getting there, so we arrived somewhat earlier than expected. But that was good, since we had to return the rental car and make sure everything was paid for (we had to pay £30 for the missing hub-cap). Besides, Marianne, who was booked on a later flight, wanted to try to get a seat on our flight, so that she could wait at Heathrow, instead of Newquay: she did succeed.

After having a cup of coffee, we checked in and waited for our flight, which, unfortunately, was delayed by half an hour. Due to this delay, at Gatwick we had to rush to catch the bus to Heathrow. But there was a mix-up, and we wound up on Air Link, instead of Speed Link, which meant that we could not go directly to Heathrow Terminal 1, but had to go to Terminal 4, where we would be picked up by a 'Help Bus' (one of the advantages of being disabled). Unfortunately, we had to wait too long, so that, by the time we got to Terminal 1, we were too late to get on our BA flight to Zurich.

Inge talked to the attendant at the check-in counter, and he sent her over to Crossair – a member of the BA group – where she was able to book seats on the nine o'clock flight to Zurich, which meant a four-hour wait. We went up to the restaurant and had something to eat, and then got in touch with Sterks to inform them of what had happened. After that, we said good-by to Marianne, whose flight to Cologne was to leave long before ours, and who wanted to do some shopping, anyway.

When we got to Zurich, it was pouring rain, and we had to wait over an hour for Herr Sterk to come. I think he was just as happy to see us as we were to see him. Finally, after we got home, we went straight to bed, since it was half past twelve and we were completely exhausted.

Chapter XI

THE CARING HANDS

The caring hands are those that serve the ill,
by tending to their needs with inborn skill,
that help to banish fear and lessen pain,
by feeling empathy in times of strain
and showing it to fortify their will.

When life demands, they comfort to instil
entrusting in the way they must fulfil
unpleasant tasks: to hurt and yet remain
the caring hands.

Although the battle is, at times, uphill,
the dedication to mankind is still
intact, the motivation to maintain
the fitting care, becalming but humane,
is always there to move the versatile,
the caring hands.

After our return from England, we slowly got used to life in Germany. In the summer of 2002, a new physiotherapist, Heidrun Grosshardt, came to me as an addition to Petra. Heidrun practiced the same therapeutic exercises with me, as did Petra. In the fall of the year 2003 Petra got married. For this reason the owner of the physical-therapeutic office, Herr Faul, hired as substitute Claudia Killmaier. Claudia continued the same exercises with me as Petra and Heidrun.

On October of 2004, after my nap, I noticed that I was not very good on my legs. I informed my wife, who notified Doctor Rogalla, who diagnosed a slight stroke and, therefore, had me taken to Friedrichshafen hospital, where I had to stay for a few days. The effect of the second stroke was not so grave, however, I noticed changes in my left arm and hand. For this reason my therapists and I changed the therapy by additional emphasis on my left side. During physical therapeutic exercises, we noticed severe attacks of dizziness during changes of position which impaired my walking. In addition I sensed more insecurity and severe weakness in my legs. Climbing stairs was, at this time, not possible. Pain in my arms and both lower legs, caused by increased ataxia, became more severe. I noticed that it had become more difficult to reach for and grasp things. Despite this I was not prepared for what came to me: stroke no. 3.

On February 24, 2005, I experienced my third stroke. This time I was well aware of it and asked my wife to call Frau Dr. Scheller. After she had examined me, she called an ambulance, which took me to the St. Elizabeth hospital in Ravensburg, to the stroke unit. Here they again discovered bleeding in the Thalamus region of my brain. After the weekend in the stroke unit, I was taken to a room with three beds of which one was vacant. The other patient had the TV running all hours of the day and night. This was one of the reasons why my mental stability deteriorated and an "I couldn't care less" feeling took over. I gave the impression that I was giving up and did not want to do anything against it. The apathy went so far that I felt neither thirsty nor hungry and only wanted to stay in bed, not willing to do anything, except therapy.

This condition lasted more than three weeks and even led my wife to assume that my end was nearing. So she informed my four brothers and sisters. My twin brother and his wife flew to Germany. The reunion was not as pleasant as it could have been because I lay very apathetic in my bed and could not really enjoy their visit.

In spite of all, I must have sensed something, since my attitude changed completely about three days after their departure. Suddenly I sensed a positive wish to do something. I do not know why, but I pulled the tubes, that fed me, out of my throat, which did not cause great joy among doctors and nurses. From then on I felt very good. My appetite for solid food as well as for liquids suddenly returned. Also my interest in life itself increased immensely.

When I was released, I reached an agreement with the senior consultant, that, instead of a further rehabilitation, I would prefer to have physiotherapy twice a week. When my wife was granted a cure after her spinal operation, and because we wanted to be together, I went with her, although I had to pay for my part of the expenses. We did not care about that, the main thing was, that we could be together. The rehabilitation took place in the "Heilig Geist Spital" in Ravensburg. This hospital was in the middle of town with possibilities for shopping, window shopping, and visiting coffee shops nearby.

The hospital had a back yard with a café under trees. We had our own room, which we enjoyed immensely. A friend of ours gave us a small TV set which we enjoyed watching every evening, since we could cuddle up while watching. The treatments we had every day, such as group gymnastics, memory training, dexterity exercises, etc. we had together which my wife thoroughly enjoyed. Our group also liked baking and we had our own products with a cup of coffee afterwards.

In addition we both had individual treatments, such as physiotherapy, walking up and down stairs, swimming and other exercises, such as ergo therapy and speech therapy for myself.

After our return home from the Heilig Geist Spital, we were visited by a representative of an emergency call center who offered us two possibilities: a wrist band or neckband type alarm button. We decided on the latter for more convenience. We had no idea whether, or how often we would use it, it was, however, very calming just to have it. Its usefulness was proven early enough. I used it for the first time on an evening when my wife fell down and could not get up by herself. Because of her osteoporosis and the dangers connected therewith, I was able to help her only by activating the emergency call button. The next time it happened, was when my wife was in the hospital and I was alone at home. About two o'clock in the morning I sensed severe pain in my legs. Because I did neither know what caused the pain nor where it came from, I thought it would go away when I calmed down. This was, of course, an error. With time the pain became stronger. Finally, at four o'clock in the morning, the pain became almost unbearable and I could not help my self other than activating the emergency call button to inform the nurse who answered my call. After I had explained my problem, she assured me that a nurse would be with me shortly. Within a quarter of an hour the nurse was there.

After she examined me she was certain that I had had an attack of gout. She prescribed medication and had it delivered by the pharmacy. All in all I activated the emergency call several times in the past seven years for me and my wife. Anyway, the emergency call system has been worth the price.

Before my wife went into the hospital for her first back operation, we had engaged a private nursing service, because I was alone at home. I had also ordered and received "Meals on Wheels". During this time I had a conversation with the second in command of this service. She expressed her doubts as to whether we would be able afford their services, which really upset me. That is why, when the nurse in Heilig Geist Spital asked us about the care we would have after our return home, we did not say anything, but asked her for suggestions. She then recommended the Social Services "Linzgau" in Markdorf. We were, and still are, more than satisfied with their services. They not only provide nursing care, but also, because of the many possibilities of helping, e.g. household help, shopping, care due to prevention, and assistance in taking walks. The longer the effects of my third stroke last, the more I need assistance from our social station.

Two years after my third stroke, I was granted grade 3 in the private nursing insurance, which was absolutely necessary. The effects of stroke number three were manifold and developed themselves very slowly, before they became very noticeable. The first problems became apparent in walking. Before the third stroke, I was able to walk 45 minutes with my physical therapist, however, after my third stroke, I was only able to walk for 10 minutes with intermittent pauses. Before that I was able to walk down and up stairs. However, as time moved on, I had to walk downstairs backwards. The next big problem was feeding myself. Also, after my third stroke, I was still independent and could feed myself. But as time moved on, I became more and more dependent on my wife's help.

One problem, which became worse, was getting from my wheel chair into the bath tub. From the very beginning, the nurse had taken position in front of me, I put my arms around her neck and then she stood up, pulled me up with her, and turned to the right, so that I could sit down on the bath tub seat and she could lift my legs into the tub. In the meantime, we have changed this routine slightly, so that the nurse, while supporting my right hip with her left hand and, holding my left hand with her right, she turns me so I can sit down. Getting out of the tub was even easier. This time we turned the chair around so that it was facing the foot end of the bath tub. The nurse then lowered the arm rest so that it became easy for me to slide from the tub seat onto the chair. Both methods made things easier for me and for the nurse.

The second big change took place in the bedroom when getting out of bed. When I lay in bed, the wheel chair was located between my bed and the window in direction of the head board. When I wanted to get up, I had to turn 180 degrees so I was able to sit. This became very dangerous because of my impaired balance. I was then able to have a long talk with my physical-therapist and we found a very simple solution. We placed the wheel chair parallel to the head end of my bed facing the foot end, I then could grip the window sill from my bed and swing myself onto the wheel chair. This enabled me to start walking out of the bedroom, which meant a great relief for me.

In the meantime this has become more difficult for me because I have become less stable on my legs, although my left arm is now my only stable support.

Chapter XII

A PERFECT WORLD

Our dreams are pictures of our world,
the way it ought to be.
So when we wish or when we hope,
a dream is what we see.

We picture what the world could be
if sin were not in us,
if progress not our only goal,
greed not our stimulus.

We see the possibilities
of what we might have done
had not the vision of the new
and modern blocked our sun.

We see a wave of tolerance,
not ordered by command,
but coming from within ourselves,
convincingly expand.

We see a fair, impartial world,
where free means really free,
where justice is for everyone,
not just for you and me.

And so we dream, and while we do,
we see reality,
pretending it's a perfect world,
the way it ought to be.

In the Spring of 2007, our neurologist, Dr. Rauber, contacted Dr. Scheller because he wanted to discuss the possibility of a depth stimulation of my brain at the clinic in Augsburg resp. Cologne. As a preparatory measure I had to make an appointment for a consultation with Dr. Rauber in Markdorf, which took place on July 4, 2007. Then we made an appointment for an MRT in the clinic in Friedrichshafen on July 25. Afterwards we made an appointment with Dr. Kroiss for July 30, in the clinic in Augsburg.

On July 30 we drove to Augsburg as arranged. First we had an appointment with Dr. Kroiss. We informed her about my health status, i.e. details which were not yet known to her. Afterwards we were joined by Prof. Dr. Naumann who explained his point of view, that the tremor on my right side could be reduced by a deep brain stimulation. However, because of the danger of paralysis, the desired use of the hand could not be achieved.

Based on the present case, he recommended not going ahead with the deep brain stimulation, because the risk of a deterioration of my condition would be too grave in his opinion. Although we were disappointed, we were grateful that he was open and honest to us. I could very well live with my situation, then and now.

Chapter XIII

REMEMBERING

It seems like only yesterday, and yet,
the memory of everything we've seen
and done in all the years since first we met
has made our lives more peaceful and serene.

Today may be another one of those,
the days that earn a place within our hearts
where fondness finds a home and slowly grows,
and peace of mind in reminiscing starts.

Remembering recalls the dreams we made
come true and lived together, just we two,
believing in us and never afraid
to take a chance on something strange or new.

Remembering relives the pleasantries
of yesterday in lasting memories.

In the year 2006 I received an invitation from my High School Class on the occasion of our 50th class reunion. Although I had reservations concerning my disability, I wanted to go at all costs. In countless emails with the class secretary, I expressed my enthusiasm for this plan.

On 29 September 2007, the day finally arrived. My physical therapist, Claudia, drove us to Zurich airport and helped us to check in, for which we were very grateful. The seats in the airplane were very narrow and the plane was filled to capacity as economy class usually goes. In spite of this, the flight was rather pleasant and fast, for which we were glad. My twin brother met us at Logan airport in Boston. From there we drove to Cape Cod, about 100 km south-east of Boston. We had originally planned to stay in Osterville until the following Saturday, and then, after the class reunion, go to my brother's house in Amherst in western Massachusetts. Then, in the next week, to tour the area around Amherst, and, at the end of the week, drive on to my sister's house near Boston. The difficulties we had coming over, showed us that our plan could not be carried out. That is why my Brother suggested that we stay the whole two weeks in Osterville, with the exception of the following Saturday, when the class reunion was scheduled to take place. His opinion was that, if the family wanted to see us, they could come to us. We were both very grateful for this suggestion because we were quite sure that we would not have been able to cope with the stress of our original plans.

In Osterville, there were difficulties, which we had to overcome in time. I was dependent on my wheel chair and could not freely move about, especially, from inside the house to the outside. The biggest problem was getting out of the house, and into the garage, since between the house and the garage were two pretty high steps. I had to get out of my wheel chair, hold on the door frame, and slowly let myself down into the garage. That was one reason, why we left the house only twice. Besides, this wonderful holiday home was so comfortable and cozy that we were able to enjoy a most wonderful and relaxing vacation.

We also enjoyed watching the many visitors in the back yard, as there were cute little chipmunks, my wife's favorites, squirrels, chickadees, and one or two cardinals.

On 6 October 2007 my brother drove us from Osterville to Ashland, to our class reunion. Obviously my brother underestimated the distance because we arrived about one hour late. This, however, had no effect on our good moods, as we noticed immediately that they were waiting for us. By the way, I was not the only one in a wheel chair.

We were able to reminisce with our class mates, but one noticed the many years in which we had not been in touch with each other. In spite of this, we were very glad to have been there. Before we left, a group picture was taken and the class secretary sent me a copy. I still enjoy looking at it from time to time.

On Sunday, 7 October, we got up early because we were expecting my youngest sister with her family, i.e. her husband, their daughter Mary with husband Nick and their three boys. My sister had baked various quiches which she brought to Osterville. These were absolutely delicious because she is a great cook and baker. After lunch we went into the living room and watched American football together. Then my brother Denny went outside to the backyard and played table tennis with our three great-nephews. It made me rather sad that I was not able to play with them. I can get along quite well with my handicaps, however, it is sometimes painful not being able to do certain things. In spite of this, I had great fun watching them. It was a wonderful reunion after ten long years.

On Saturday the 12th Linda's son, Christopher with his wife Cathy and their daughters Katy and Kerrin surprised us with their visit. We were very happy to meet Chris's family at last. We were very sorry that we met them practically at the last minute because the next day we were to fly back to Germany.

On Sunday 13 October we left Osterville and drove to Boston airport. We had seats in the middle row up front. The flight was uneventful since it was at night.

When we arrived in Zurich, we had an unpleasant surprise. When we got on the plane in Boston, the stewardess removed by accident one arm rest as well as the cushion I had been sitting on. On our arrival in Zurich we had to go to the insurance desk of the airline to put in a claim for the missing items. After this delay, we could finally move on to the exit. A friend had promised to pick us up, however, we waited in vain. After two hours of waiting, a limousine which wanted to pick up passengers stopped by and the driver offered to drive us home because his passengers had not shown up. After a short discussion we agreed on a fare. Although the trip was anything but cheap, we were very glad that we had finally gotten home.

Chapter XIV

ONE ALONE

To live alone appears to be ideal:
one does the things one wants, is on one's own,
and is convinced that it can help to heal,
to live alone.

For one believes one somehow can atone
for an offence against oneself and feel
relief by living by oneself, unknown
to others and unwilling to reveal
the reasons for the wind that one has sown,
but there are times when it's a grim ordeal
to live alone.

In the spring of 2008 my wife detected a lump in her left breast. Since this meant an alarm signal for her, she immediately made an appointment with our doctor. In the X-ray it showed that there was a tumor which needed to be operated. Our problem, of course was, that I would need to be cared for during her absence from home. We discussed this with our family doctor and she recommended that we inform ourselves of the possibility of a short term stay in a nursing home not too far from our home. We contacted this place and made an arrangement for the end of June 2008. At the same time my wife made an appointment for an operation with the clinic in Friedrichshafen.

On 30 June 2008 we drove to the nursing home because my wife was to have her operation on 1 July. We were very surprised that the nursing home had planned a summer night party for that evening. There was a lot to eat and drink and we all felt very happy and relaxed. The personnel of the home was in charge of food, drink and service. In the course of the evening they took me around the house and showed me where I would live during the next five weeks. It took five weeks because three operations became necessary before the tumors could be completely removed. After each operation my wife had to wait until it could be determined how they were to continue. That is why I was not released until August 5, 2008.

My stay in Wespach was not unpleasant, however, not quite my cup of tea. I had a very good relationship with the personnel, however, there was not enough time for lengthy discussions because we spent too much time in the dining room. We had additional activities such as physiotherapy and singing folksongs. In the afternoon we had coffee and cake. Once we were served in my room because it was our wedding anniversary on that day.

Two activities I really enjoyed were, first of all, the audio book of Dan Brown's bestseller, "The Da Vinci Code", which my brother had given me on his last visit. I finished the book within one week in which I did not have to stay in the dining room so very long. The second activity was going for walks around the small pond, which lasted a good hour.

Unfortunately, the relationship with the other inhabitants could not be maximized because most of them were dement patients. However, I got along with most of them quite well, although the slight communication problem proved to be an insurmountable hindrance. Despite this, many of the patients seemed to be rather sad when I left.

Chapter XV

MOURNING SKY

The clouds that cloak the sky today
are clad in deepest, darkest grey,
perhaps because they feel the pain
of loss that I must bear, and rain,
to weep with me in sympathy,
partaking in my agony.

In summer of 2007 our sister-in-law, Marianne, became very ill and during an examination at the hospital the doctors diagnosed cancer of the red blood cells. In the course of the following year, the illness became worse and Marianne stayed in bed most of the day. She seemed to have lost her will to live. It became so bad that my wife became so worried that she decided to travel to Cologne for Marianne's 69th birthday. She went by train instead of by car because she was alone, since my illness became worse and, therefore, it had become impossible for me to travel with her. We therefore decided to apply for care during my wife's absence, which was approved.

According to my wife, the trip to Cologne was quite pleasant and Marianne and her younger son Thomas met her at the railway station. It seemed that my wife's visit was very good for Marianne, she did not stay in bed all day and even went out for coffee with friends. She even went shopping and to the theater. It seemed that she found a new interest in life, which made us very happy. In spite of this, her condition made us very worried.

In the course of the following months our worries were confirmed. At the end of May 2009, she was taken to the hospital and passed away on June 1st.

Since it was, in our opinion, too much of a strain for my wife to travel the whole distance to Cologne alone, our oldest nephew Christoph had made an arrangement with a taxi company in Cologne to pick us up and take us back after the funeral. The trip was very pleasant and we arrived rather relaxed. The preparations for the funeral were quite strenuous for my wife, but she mastered them quite well. The funeral was very well organized and the undertaker had made all the necessary arrangements, including those for my wheel chair. Because of the length of Marianne's illness and her suffering, there was more of a sense of relief rather than of sadness during the meal after the funeral.

On Friday 12 June, we drove with Christoph and Thomas back to Bermatingen. The trip was uneventful and we were very pleased to be at home again. However, during the night something rather strange happened. We heard loud voices coming from the room of Christoph and Thomas. My wife went into their room where our two nephews were shouting at each other and she asked Christoph to sleep in another room. Since his mother passed away, Thomas slept very restlessly, which he could not explain and for which he could not find a solution. For this reason he had to undergo psychiatric treatment after his return to Cologne. His condition has improved since then, however, he is still not back to his old self.

Chapter XVI

GUARDIAN ANGEL

Because I once sustained a stroke,
and suffer still beneath its yoke,
need aid and comfort constantly,
my loved one watches over me.

She's never thought to question why
the fates chose me to brutify,
for, since she vowed fidelity,
my loved one watches over me.

The way is long, at times not fair,
is often more than I can bear,
and still, through all uncertainty,
my loved one watches over me.

I'm proud to have her by my side,
but most of all I'm gratified
that fervently, but tenderly,
my loved one watches over me.

My life is wonderful with her,
no matter what may yet occur,
the essence of that life will be:
my loved one watches over me.

In the meantime, my wife had several situations in which I had to activate the emergency call for help. These incidences were, as earlier described, occasions in which my wife, due to a sudden feeling of weakness, fell down and could not get up by herself. Although these weaknesses were not caused directly by her osteoporosis, they could have caused serious injuries. In the future, we must be very careful, especially when we are not in the same room, respectively, when she tries to do too much at the same time, without thinking it over.

Another health problem is her knees which have become affected by deterioration. An orthopedic specialist suggested several times that she have a knee operation, but she refused every time, after thorough consideration, because, in her opinion, the danger was too great She had occupied herself with the subject very long and in great detail, and knows it quite well. Of course, the fear of possible permanent injuries played an important role in her considerations, even if the orthopedist did not seem it possible. There are too many examples of such injuries that one could neglect them. My wife's reasoning was that, if she should become permanently disabled, she would not be able to care for me. For this reason I am convinced that my wife should maintain her negative opinion.

Since her breast cancer operation two years ago, my wife has to go regularly for check-ups at the clinic. So far these checkups have been positive from the patient's point of view. These checkups take place within three years after the last operation.

Since that time my wife has great difficulties in sleeping, especially, when the moon is full or when it snows or when there is south wind (German: Föhn), although science maintains that this is impossible.

Sometimes she cannot sleep at all, or falls asleep very late. The rescue comes in that the alarm clock goes off at seven o'clock, I hold her head in both my hands and she immediately falls asleep. The funny thing is that she has no problems falling asleep when we cuddle. This relaxes me and makes very happy and proud that I can at least do my part to solve this problem.

On May 7 of this year, my wife had a slight stroke. Luckily the nurse of the Linzgau station was with me at that time so she could take my wife to her bed and call the emergency medic. She examined my wife and gave her nitro spray and she suggested that my wife stay in bed until our family doctor could come. The result of the doctor's examination the next day was that my wife's blood pressure was too high. She prescribed a light pressure reducing medicine. Since then my wife's blood pressure has caused no more problems. Nevertheless, since then she checks her blood pressure regularly, just to be on the safe side.

Although I was a very heavy smoker, I was very lucky that I was able to quit in the year 1991. My wife, however, smoked until October 2008. For health reasons, and, above all, for financial considerations, my wife decided to quit smoking. At first she had slight problems but in time she resigned herself to the new situation, and even when she feels the urge, she does not give in.

A much bigger problem for my wife is the fact that we live on the second floor, which means that we have to walk many steps up and down stairs, when we have something to take care of outside. Because of her osteoporosis she is always fearful that she may stumble or fall and break her bones. There is always the fear of falling which we both have.

In July 2009 we had been thinking of selling our car. We asked our nephews to take care of it by finding a buyer for us. The result was that friends and acquaintances of our nephews drove the car without real interest in buying it. We then took back the contract to sell our car and, although we drive the car very little, there are situations in which we need the car, above all when my wife has doctors' appointments. She is still a safe driver and I have no qualms about letting her continue to drive.

Chapter XVII

ON WINGS OF FAITH

Sail on, my friend, on wings of faith.
Although the way be dark and dense,
you need not fear misfortune's wraith,
for guidance comes from Providence.

Although the way be dark and dense,
it leads you to your destiny,
for guidance comes from Providence:
the light of true security.

It leads you to your destiny,
revealing risk and obstacle,
the light of true security,
your omnipresent miracle.

Revealing risk and obstacle,
its major task, moves you to trust
your omnipresent miracle,
convinced that its intents are just.

Its major task moves you to trust
the voice inside yourself as well,
convinced that its intents are just
as righteous as your feelings tell.

The voice inside yourself as well,
the conscience that can make your quest
as righteous as your feelings tell,
can put your credence to the test.

The conscience that can make your quest
an ideal for the hesitant
can put your credence to the test,
and so, be brave and vigilant.

An ideal for the hesitant,
you need not fear misfortune's wraith,
and so, be brave and vigilant:
sail on, my friend, on wings of faith.

With my first stroke Diabetes also came, although I had never had problems with blood sugar before. In the beginning, in the hospital in Überlingen, I was given 16 units of insulin, which were reduced to eight units within six weeks. Since my transfer from Überlingen to Gailingen, I no longer needed insulin injections. My diabetes was regularly checked and I had no more problems.

One problem I had long before my first stroke, was high blood pressure, mainly the diastolic pressure was often over 100. Before my first stroke I weighed over 100 kilograms, which in the course of six weeks in Überlingen were reduced to below eighty kilograms, since I was put on a diet from the beginning. My blood pressure as well as my blood sugar level has had to be checked at least once a week, during hospital stays, daily.

Since my third stroke, the number of physiotherapy hours has remained the same, twice per week with two different therapists. However, the exercises have basically changed. First the therapist does movement exercises with my arms and legs in sitting. When the weather is bad, we walk from my office to the kitchen (about 12 meters) and back. When the weather is dry, we walk on the balcony outside my office, back and forth, about 36 meters with breaks. With my second therapist I first walk from my office to the kitchen, respectively on the balcony. Several massage exercises then follow, to relax my muscles.

Although I have written very few poems since my third stroke, I have very often taken older poems for competitions and, although none of them has won, many were short-listed. These partial successes gave me enough incentive to keep taking part in competitions.

The most positive of these negative experiences was, the fact that I could stop my compulsive gambling, which had lasted several years. The causes were actually unimportant because they were manifold but, in spite of this, they are surmountable if one wants to, which I apparently did not. Funnily enough, I never felt the urge to gamble since my first stroke, even when I happened to be near a slot machine. Now, after almost fifteen years, I am certain that I have left the addiction behind me and that the danger no longer exists. This may sound paradoxical, yet reason enough to be grateful for my strokes.

One of the most important things in my life is the correct philosophy of life. For years I have always asked myself: "Is it important?" If the answer was "No!", I stopped concerning myself with an answer. Life is too short to occupy oneself with unimportant matters. The humor in my life is actually just as important. I have often been asked how, in such a situation, I can be so cheerful and humorous. The main object is to distinguish between seriousness and fun, because the illness is too serious a matter, not to be able to laugh about it.

Chapter XVIII

THAT YOU

I love that you,
the one I see first thing,
who smiles and kisses me
with words of love,
before she cuddles close,.
head resting on my hands,
to doze away for just a while.

I love that you,
the one who misses me
whenever we're apart,
no matter what
the distance or the time,
and deeply sighs relief
when we're together once again.

I love that you,
the one who takes my hand
and guides me through this life
who gives me strength
by taking care of me
and always being there
with faith and hope for both of us.

I love that you,
the one who loves me, too,
and will until the end,
as once we vowed,
so many years ago,
and honour for all time,
in simple words, 'I love that you'.

When I came to Germany as a soldier with the US Army, it did not take long until, out of curiosity and for philosophical reasons, I spent more of my free time in and around Crailsheim than in the barracks. It did not take long until I met a young lady and we fell in love. On 10 August 1959 I proposed and, of course, she said "yes". I then wrote to my parents in the States to tell them that I had become engaged. My mother's reply did not surprise me, she wrote "You are now 19, when you get married before you are 25, the marriage won't last!" We got married when I was 22 und we have been waiting for over 48 years for it not to work out, we must have been doing something wrong.

But my mother was not the only person against our marriage. My wife's parents as well as some members of the army looked for ways to torpedo our plans. The only result was that we got closer and closer. We became even happier in the long run than if everything had run smoothly.

After three years of college and four years of experience in the U.S.A., we decided to go back to Germany. During our vacation there in May, 1969, I was offered the opportunity to have an interview with an American firm in Düsseldorf.

The agreement was that I should contact them when and if I return to Germany. We moved to Germany in January 1970, and I worked for this company for four years. The problem was that the company was located in Düsseldorf while we had our apartment in Cologne. I tried to find either a job in Cologne or an apartment in Düsseldorf. We finally landed in the Black Forest in southern Germany in 1974.

Unfortunately, the years that followed were ones of little success and joblessness. In all these years my wife was the support that a husband needed. Finally I found the position I had really been looking for: I became an English teacher for industrial companies in Germany. This positive situation lasted eight years until my first stroke. In this time and in the following fifteen years, I am very grateful for my wife's love and support.

During my stay in Gailingen early 1996, I had several conversations with a fellow patient that made me fully aware of my confidence in my wife. He and his wife had been on vacation in Spain. The weather was very beautiful, and they decided to stay until the last day of their vacation and then drive home in one night. They agreed to take turns at the wheel, the husband drove first. After the first change, the wife drove and he lay down in the back of the car. A thunderstorm came up and the wife lost control of the car. Amazingly, the wife was not injured, but the husband had become paralyzed on one side of his body. Within six months after this accident, the wife filed for divorce, and got it. She could not accept the responsibility of having to take care of her invalid husband for the rest of his life. He told me himself that his wife was too sensitive and that he did not want to burden her.

Although the danger of divorce never existed for us, this story made me realize how well I have fared with my wife. In spite of her own, already mentioned, handicaps, she was always by my side, i.e. in all areas such as care, physiotherapy, ergo-therapy or speech therapy. She has always supported me in every way. For this reason I love her and I always will. For this reason, giving up has never been an alternative for me.

Glossary

Aneurysm:	localized dilatation of a blood vessel, particularly an artery, or the heart
Ataxia:	lack of coordination of the voluntary muscles resulting in irregular movements of the body
BFA:	(Bundesversicherungsanstalt für Angestellte) the german association for social insurance
Computertomography:	computer supported x-ray with a high level of dispersion
Diabetes:	chronic disorder involving Insulin
Ergotherapy:	is medication for the motoric
Hypoxia:	lack of oxygen in the tissue
Magnetic resonance tomography:	(MRI) is an image producing process in medicine for the depiction of structures and functions of organs in the body.
Logopedia:	speech therapy
Nitro spray:	spray for inhalation for vascular dilatation

Orthopedics:	treatement of the support and movement apparatus
Osteoporosis:	is an aging of the bones which makes them susceptible to breakage
Paresis:	paralysis
Plegien:	complete paralysis of the skeleton muscles
Stroke Unit:	neurological observation station
depth stimulation:	it is a medical operation in the brain
Tremor:	trembling
Tutor:	teaching aid by a student or teacher

ACKNOWLEDGEMENT

For the invaluable assistance in the preparation of this book I would like to express my gratitude and appreciation to the following persons and institutions:

Dr. Iris Scheller and Dr. Dorothea Rogalla, for their professional treatment and advice.

Dr. Alois Rauber, Neurologist, for his honest evaluation.

Dr. Kroiss and Prof. Dr. Naumann, Klinikum Augsburg for their open and honest evaluation of my situation.

My physiotherapists Petra Litzenburger, Claudia Killmaier and Heidrun Grosshardt, for their active and valuable assistance in getting me on my feet, as well as Heike Swysen for the information on the Bobath method.

All the nurses and the neighborly help of our Sozialstation "Linzgau" in Markdorf for exceptional care and assistance over 5 years.

The Schmieder Clinics in Gailingen and Allensbach for their exceptional rehabilitation.

The nursing home Wespach for providing a home for me for 5 weeks.

Thanks also to my family in the U.S.A. and Scotland for moral and financial support over the past years.

Mrs Sonngard Christmann for her exceptional and, sometimes, uncanny cooperation without which this book would never have been finished.

My wife Ingeborg for her love and care, without which my life would have been unbearable.

Table of Contenets